KING MIDAS

A Tale of Wisdom

Adapted by Jennifer Boudart
Illustrated by Kristen Goeters

PUBLICATIONS INTERNATIONAL, LTD.

There once was a rich king named Midas, who ruled a magical land of roses and sunshine. Midas was rich beyond imagination, but he was selfish and foolish. Instead of enjoying the warm sunshine and wonderful flowers in his beautiful kingdom, Midas spent his days locked in a room all by himself, counting his money.

There was nothing that Midas would rather do than count his riches. His gold made him feel important, and he loved to surround himself with it. Each morning King Midas headed straight to his vault. And each night he would lie awake and dream of how to get more gold.

King Midas had a beautiful daughter named Marygold. She was very different from her father. Marygold did not care much for gold, and she was not selfish at all. Day after day Marygold would walk happily among the roses in the garden. She loved taking care of all the beautiful flowers and watering them so they would grow to be even taller than she was. There was nothing Marygold liked better than smelling the sweet scent of the roses and watching the pretty butterflies.

Marygold was sorry that her father never joined her in the garden. She wished he would leave his gold and come outside to enjoy the beautiful garden.

One day Midas was counting his gold when a stranger appeared. "How did you get in here?" asked King Midas.

"I have some magical powers," said the stranger. "You sure have a lot of gold."

"Yes, but I could always use more," Midas said.

"I could give you the power to turn all that you touch into gold," said the stranger. "Would you like that?"

"Yes! Yes! Of course I would," Midas excitedly said to the mysterious stranger. "I would like that very much!"

"Very well," said the stranger. "After the next sunrise, anything you touch will turn to gold."

King Midas spent that night sitting by the window and waiting for the sun to rise. When it did, he reached to push away the curtain, and it turned into solid gold! Then Midas grabbed his chair, and it turned to gold, too! The king ran from room to room, and all that he touched turned to gold—tables, doors, mirrors, and paintings.

Then Midas rushed from his castle into Marygold's garden. He knew that this was his daughter's favorite place. Midas laid his hands on a rose, and it turned from scarlet red to gold. How delighted Marygold will be, he thought and then he turned all the roses to gold

Soon the king's stomach began to rumble. Making gold had made him so hungry! Midas returned to his castle and ordered a delicious breakfast.

Servants brought plates full of fruit, bread, meat, and eggs. King Midas decided to start with a strawberry, but when he touched it, the strawberry changed to gold and could not be eaten. Then he grabbed a goblet of water and raised it to his lips, but the water turned to gold, too! Midas was dizzy with hunger. He wanted some food, but it all turned to gold!

Suddenly Marygold came into the room, holding a gold rose and crying.

Marygold sat at the royal table and sobbed. "Look at this poor rose," she cried. "How could this have happened?"

"I made it happen!" answered King Midas. "Don't you like it?"

"My roses are ruined!" exclaimed Marygold. "They no longer smell sweet, they no longer feel like velvet, and they no longer make the butterflies dance. They are worthless!"

Like all fathers, King Midas hated to see his daughter unhappy, and he wanted to make her feel better. He rushed over to give her a comforting hug. As soon as he did, Marygold turned into solid gold!

King Midas ran from his golden daughter. He now knew his wish had been a curse, not a blessing.

Just then the mysterious stranger returned and asked, "Aren't you pleased with all your gold?"

"I was very foolish," King Midas answered. "Save my daughter, and you can have all of my gold."

"I do not want your gold, Midas. I wanted to teach you a lesson. To get your daughter back, go to the river by the rose garden. Dive into its waters and gather enough water to sprinkle over the things you have turned to gold. They will all return to normal."

King Midas called all his servants. "Gather every pail and bucket you can find," he shouted. Without another word he ran to the river's edge and leaped into the cold, rushing water.

The water around the king began to turn golden yellow. Midas watched as the golden layer fell to the bottom of the river. Quickly King Midas and his servants filled several pails with water and returned to the castle. He went straight to the dining hall and splashed water over every golden object he saw, including his daughter. As Marygold changed back to her normal self, his heart filled with joy.

King Midas was very thankful to have his daughter back. Together they went outside and changed all the gold flowers back to beautiful red roses. King Midas had learned that there are more important things in life than gold.

From that day on, King Midas was happier than he had ever been before. He no longer spent his days locked away all by himself. Instead he liked to go outdoors, where he could see the true beauty of flowers, butterflies, and his most valuable treasure, Marygold.

The only gold that King Midas cared for now was the golden sunshine.

One to Grow On
Wisdom

Wisdom is learning to make the right choices. This story shows us that it is not always easy to do the wise thing. King Midas loved gold and thought the more he had, the happier he would be.

A wise person knows that money or gold can't buy happiness and that simple things can be the best. In the end King Midas grew wiser. He discovered that gold did not make him happy and that the best things in life — his daughter, flowers, and the sunshine — are free.